This book belongs to

....

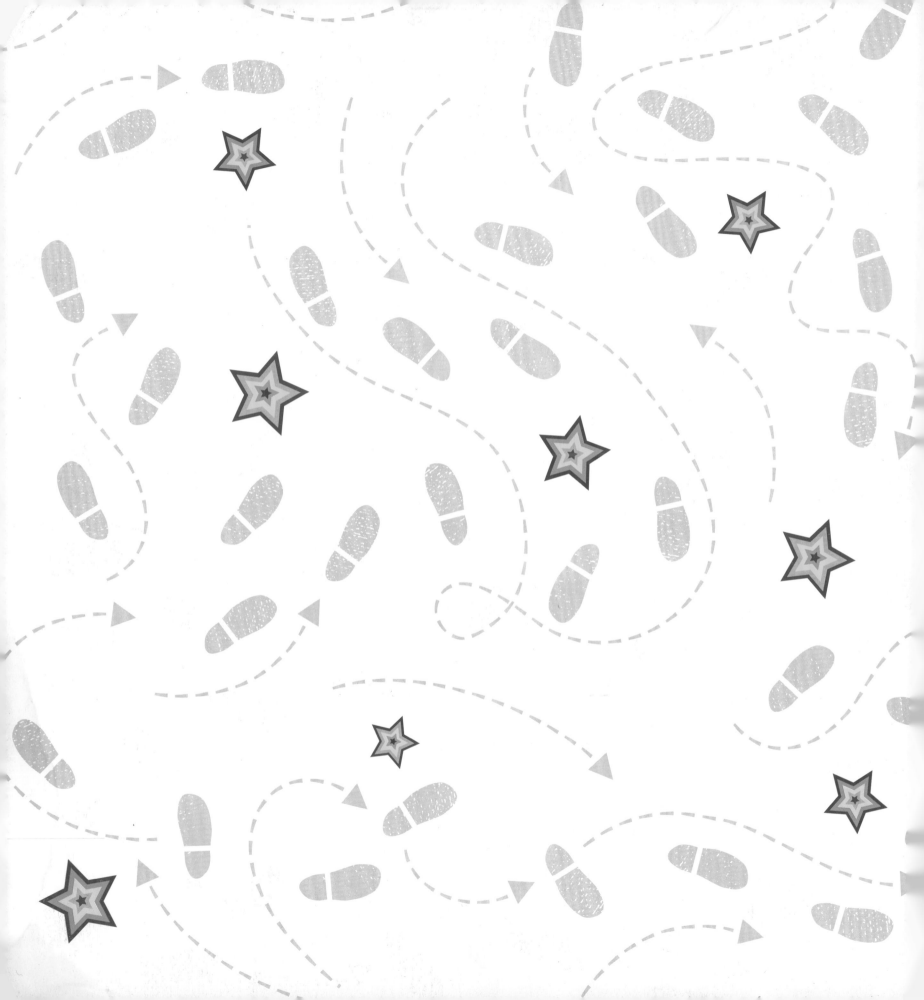

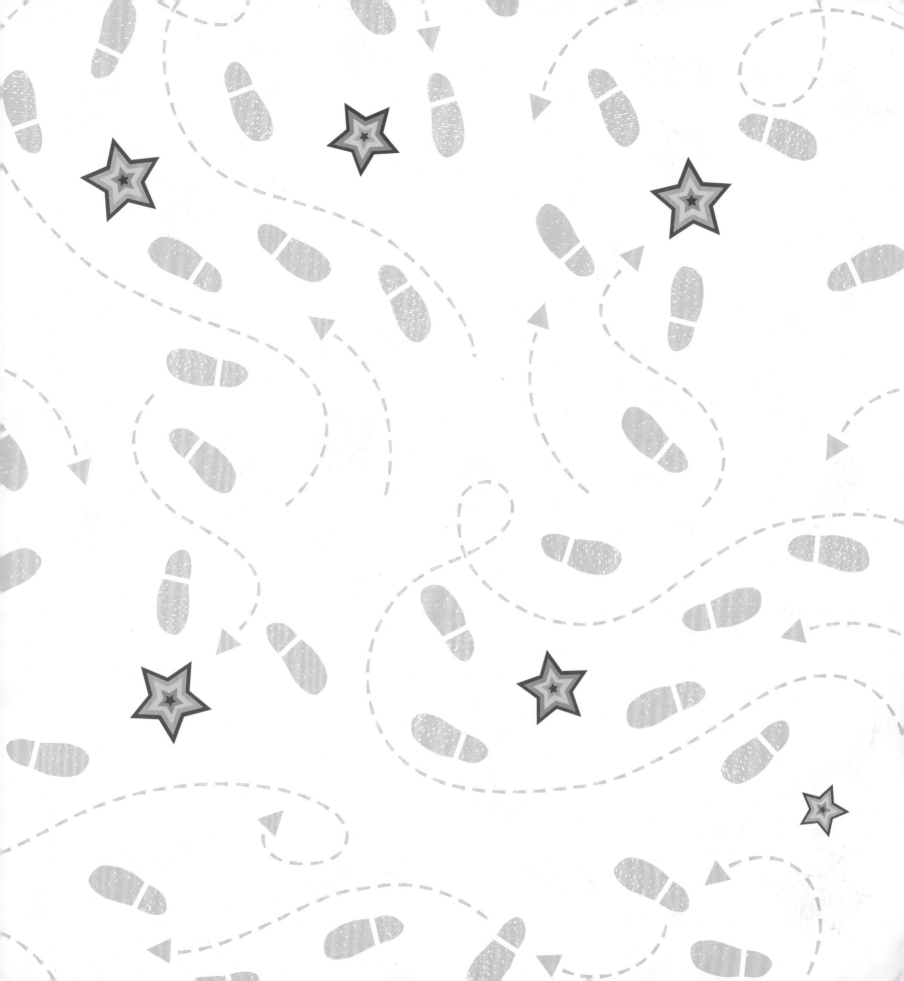

www.makebelieveideas.com

Written by Rosie Greening.
Illustrated by Stuart Lynch.

GrooViCorns
in the
City

Rosie Greening • Stuart Lynch

make
believe
ideas

This group was called the
GROOVICORNS,
and when you saw their moves,
you couldn't help but join the fun
and get into the groove!

One sunny day, an **acorn** note came for the **dancing troop**, from a **squirrel** in the **city** who knew the **groovy** group.

"It won't take long!" cried out the group.

"We'll cheer them with our dancing,

LET'S DANCE!

TV GUIDE

and hopefully be back in time
to watch Strictly Come Prancing!"

They **left** their Funky Forest friends and jumped on board a **ferry**. They were off to **help out** Squirrel and to make Moanhattan **merry**!

S.S. Groove

Moanhattan City

Beep! Beep! Beep! Beep!

But when they reached the city, it was much **worse** than they'd feared.

"Where's the sunshine?"

"What's that smell?"

"It's really grey and weird!"

The worst bit was the gloomycorns who acted like machines.

They never smiled . . .

or said hello . . .

. . . they just stared at their screens!

They found a square with glaring screens
all going flicker-flash.

MANE SQUARE

WIFI!

MORE DATA

MOVIES

They took a breath,
cried, "6, 7, 8 . . ."
and then began to . . .

The gloomycorns bumped into them, distracted by their phones. "They won't look up!" cried Ziggy, with a big, un-groovy groan.

They went down to the **subway**, where the gloomycorns looked **bored.**
But with all the **screens** and **headphones**, every dance move was **ignored!**

They breakdanced, flossed and did the dab, but no **routine** would do.

The gloomycorns were in the **cloud**, and **nothing** could get through.

"This is hopeless!" cried the group.
"Those screens are all they see."

So they sadly trotted off
to visit Squirrel in her tree.

Dough-nut
(smile)

Moanhattan
Park

Squirrel said, "Don't worry, guys –
you tried your best, I know.
Could you teach me some dance moves
before you have to go?"

So the groovicorns explained their steps, and Squirrel had such fun,
that she filmed them on her acorn phone . . .

Step left … turn around …
hands in the air …
step right … star jump!

… to **watch** once they were done.

When they watched the video,
it filled them all with cheer.
It was happy, fun and colourful
and gave them an idea . . .

They posted it on HoofTube
and as **quickly** as can be,

it appeared on **every screen**
for **all** the gloomycorns to see!

All across the city, everybody learnt the moves, and the gloomycorns put down their phones to get into the groove.

There was **singing** in the subways . . .

. . . and **swirling** in the street.

The gloomycorns were having **fun** and **dancing** to the beat!

After that, Moanhattan shone with laughter, life and colour, as the gloomycorns all learnt to laugh and talk to one another.

And **back at home,** the groovicorns were keeping **busy,** too.

They were **filming** groovy **dances** . . .

...for EVERYONE to do!

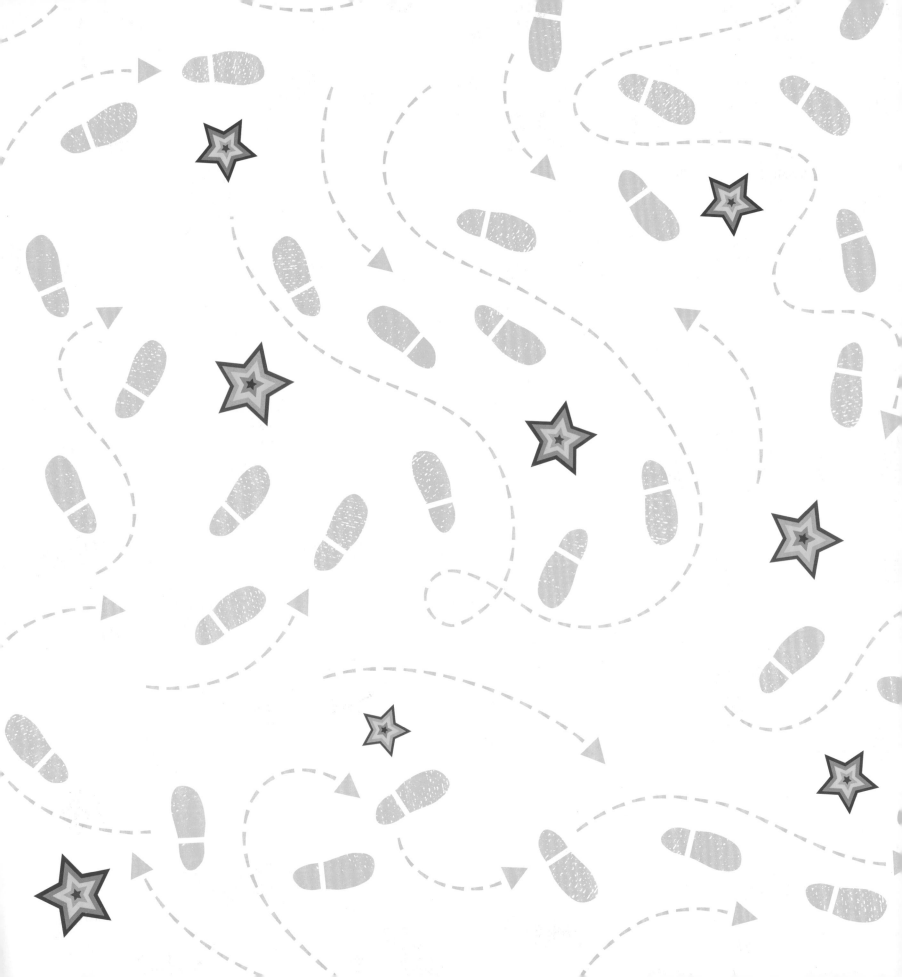

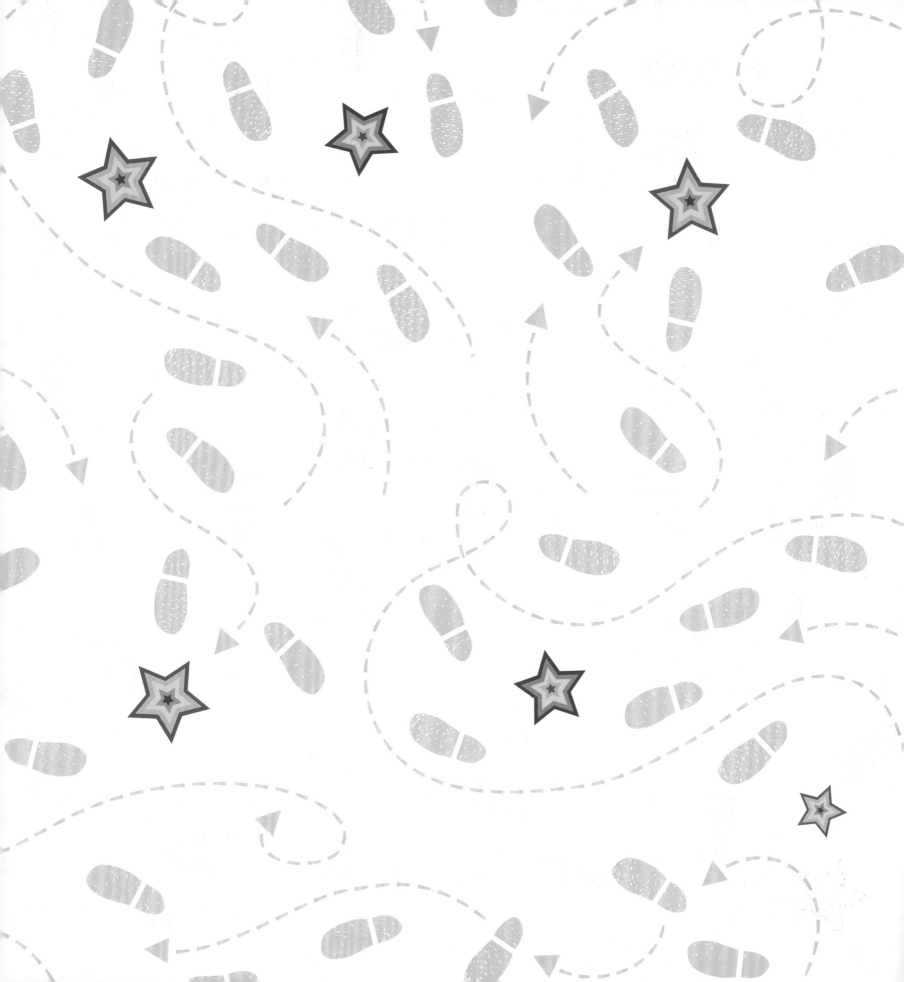